Mucky Pup's Christmas

Written and illustrated by
Ken Brown

Ⓐ

Andersen Press
London

Mucky Pup
was busy being helpful. He collected the post,

sampled the cake,

For Janice

Copyright © 1998 by Ken Brown
The rights of Ken Brown to be identified as the author and illustrator of this work
have been asserted by him in accordance with the Copyright, Designs and Patents Act, 1988.
First published in Great Britain in 1998 by Andersen Press Ltd., 20 Vauxhall Bridge Road,
London SW1V 2SA. Published in Australia by Random House Australia Pty.,
20 Alfred Street, Milsons Point, Sydney, NSW 2061. All rights reserved.
Colour separated by Fotoriproduzioni Grafiche, Verona.
Printed and bound in Italy by Grafiche AZ, Verona.

10   9   8   7   6   5   4   3   2   1

British Library Cataloguing in Publication Data available.

ISBN 0 86264 845 9

This book has been printed on acid-free paper

and rearranged the tree. Clever Mucky Pup!

No-one else thought he was clever.
"Bad, *bad* Mucky Pup! You've spoilt the Christmas cards."
"You've spoilt the Christmas cake."
"You've spoilt the Christmas tree."
"And it's Christmas tomorrow!
Out! Out of the house!"

Mucky Pup went to find Pig.

"What's up?" said Pig.
"They don't want me," said Mucky Pup miserably.
"They say I've spoilt this Christmas thing.
Do you know what it is, Pig?"

Pig didn't know. Nor did Horse or Hen or Duck.
Cat *said* she knew but wasn't telling.
"It doesn't sound much fun whatever it is," said Pig.
"Cheer up, Mucky Pup. Stay here with us tonight."

So Mucky Pup snuggled down in the soft, warm straw with Pig.
He thought he could hear someone calling his name,
but perhaps it was just a dream.

The next morning,
everything was clean and white and new.
"Do you think it's the Christmas thing, Pig?" asked Mucky Pup.
"Can't be," said Pig. "It looks too much fun.
Come on, Mucky Pup. Let's play!"

And that's what they did . . .

They skated,

they snowballed,

they sledged and . . .

Wheeeeeeeeee . . .

"Mucky Pup! *Clever* Mucky Pup —

you found us! We've called and called.
Don't you know? It's Christmas Day!"

And they put him on the sled and went back to
the warm, bright house, where Mucky Pup
at last found out what Christmas was.
There were parcels, and paper,
and his very own present . . .

. . . and it was *lots* of fun.

"I didn't spoil Christmas after all,"
thought Mucky Pup happily.
"I shall tell Pig tomorrow!"